It is a hot summer day on Dino Ranch. Min, Miguel, and Jon are out and about helping the dinosaurs keep happy and cool.

Lending a hand is their job, after all. They're the Dino Ranchers!

Jon has just ridden over to the brontosauruses' watering hole when he realizes something is wrong.

"The hot weather has made the water level too low," he says. "The baby brontos can't reach it."

DINO RANCH

Pterodactyl Attack!

ADAPTED BY **MEREDITH RUSU**

SCHOLASTIC INC.

ISBN 978-1-338-69223-5

10 9 8 7 6 5 4 3 2 1   22 23 24 25 26

Printed in the U.S.A.   40

First printing 2022

Book design by **Ashley Vargas**

"Howdy, rancheroos!" calls their dad. "Is everything okay?"

"No, Pa," says Min. "The water level is low, and the young ones can't reach the creek."

"Hmmm," says Pa. "That's a problem we'll need to solve."

"I have an idea!" says Miguel with a big grin. "We could build a dam. That would stop the water and make the creek higher."

"Good thinking!" says Pa. "Let's get to work."

The Dino Ranchers follow Miguel's plan.
They cut logs and nail them together to build a
sturdy dam.
"Okay, Goliath!" Miguel calls to a tall
brontosaurus. "Lift it into place!"

The dam blocks the creek just like Miguel had hoped. Soon, the water level is high enough for the baby brontos to drink.

"Now *all* of our brontosauruses can drink fresh water," Min says happily.

"Miguel, your plans are always dino-mite!" cheers Jon.

Little do the Dino Ranchers know, water isn't the only thing the dam is blocking!

A bunch of floating vanilly pads have gotten stuck behind the dam, too.

Vanilly pads are wild pterodactyls' favorite food. Usually, the flowers float downstream for the mamas to gather for their babies.

But because of the dam, the pterodactyls can't reach them.

And without vanilly pads, the pterodactyls are *very* hungry.

That afternoon, Jon, Miguel, and Min are finishing their chores when they see dozens of wild pterodactyls swooping down from the sky. "Dino Ranchers—run!" shouts Jon.

Pterodactyls snatch up the triceratops' turnips!
They grab the apatosauruses' apples!
They even snag the Dino Ranchers' lunch!
"Not Ma's apple pies!" cries Miguel.

"Wild pterodactyls never come to the ranch for food," says Min. "Why are they here?"

"I don't know," says Miguel. "But I have a plan to scare them away. We'll build a scare-o-dactyl!"

Quickly, the friends
follow Miguel's
plan and build a
giant pterodactyl
scarecrow.

"It's ptero-scaro
time!" says Miguel.

But . . . Miguel's
idea doesn't go
according to
plan. Instead of
being scared, the
pterodactyls think
the scare-o-dactyl
is hungry, too. They
try to feed it!

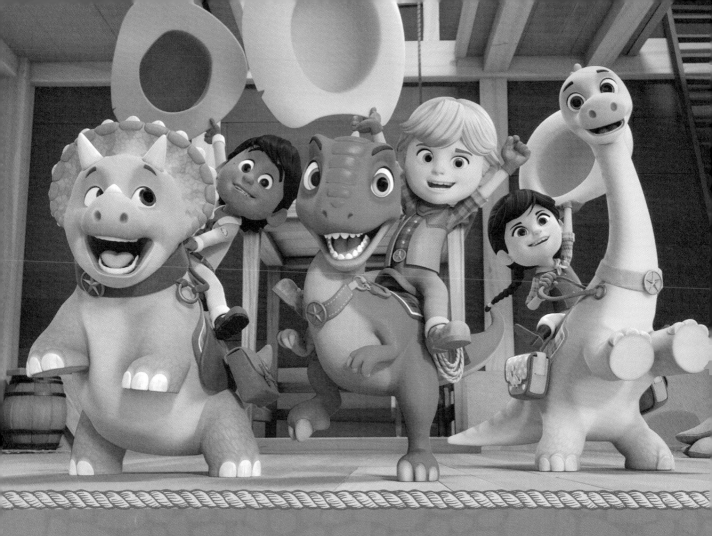

"I don't get it," says Jon. "Why would wild pterodactyls want our food? Don't they usually eat vanilly pads from the creek?"

Miguel's eyes light up. "They sure do! Maybe if we gather a bunch of those, we can lure them off the ranch. Let's ride!"

When the rancheroos reach the creek, they finally realize what's happening.

"The vanilly pads are all stuck behind my new dam!" says Miguel.

"No wonder the pterodactyls are so hungry," says Min. "Our dam has stopped them from eating their favorite food."

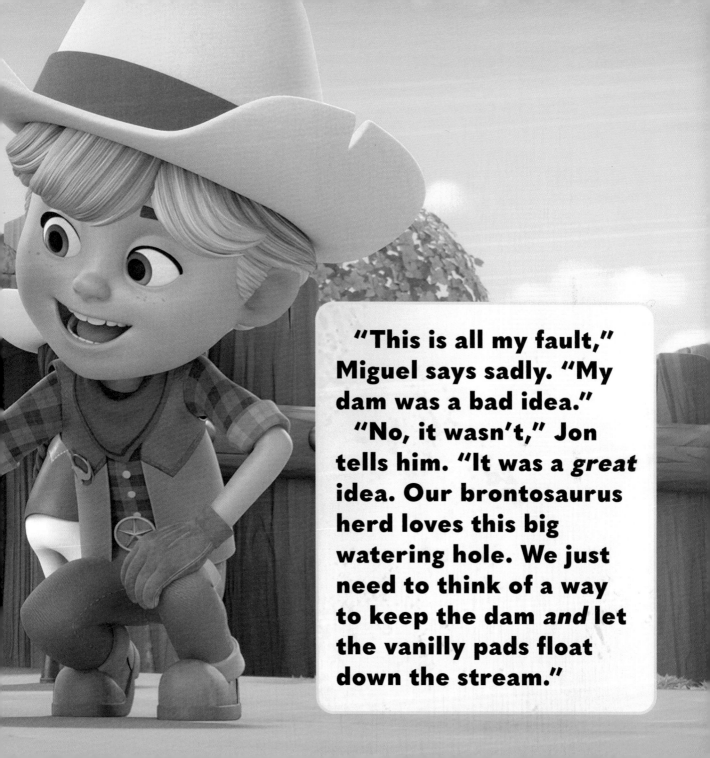

"This is all my fault," Miguel says sadly. "My dam was a bad idea."

"No, it wasn't," Jon tells him. "It was a *great* idea. Our brontosaurus herd loves this big watering hole. We just need to think of a way to keep the dam *and* let the vanilly pads float down the stream."

"You're right," says Miguel. "In fact, you just gave me an even better idea!"

Miguel quickly sketches his new plan. "Let's get to work!"

Using a saw, nails, and a bit of creativity, the Dino Ranchers add a wheel-powered door to the center of the dam.

It should be just big enough to let the vanilly pads through. But will it work?

It does! With the door open, the vanilly pads float right through while still keeping the water level high enough for the baby brontos to drink.

"Miguel, you did it!" cheer Jon and Min. "Now the brontos can drink *and* the pterodactyls can eat!"

Soon, the wild pterodactyls have plenty of vanilly pads again. They fly home from Dino Ranch, happy to be back where they belong.

"Your plan really saved the day," Jon tells Miguel. "It took a few tries." Miguel grins. "But I guess sometimes you need a good plan to go wrong in order for a great plan to go right!"

JON

MIN

MIGUEL

 BLITZ

 CLOVER

 TANGO

DINO RANCH

DINO RANCH

DINO RANCH

DINO RANCH

DINO RANCH

DINO RANCH

MIGUEL

Inventor

Miguel is a super-smart inventor, always thinking up new gadgets to help out along the ranch. He likes to take his time and is always careful wherever there is danger. When a problem pops up, Miguel is ready to invent a way to solve it!

MIN

Dino-Doctor

The gang's most vocal cheerleader, Min is a dino-doctor in training. Together with Clover, Min always knows just what to do to help a dino in distress. Her dino-care cases are packed with everything that she and Clover need to help cure a dinosaur on the fly.

JON

Dino Trainer

As the oldest sibling, Jon is being groomed as the ranch's dino trainer. Fun and fearless, he loves adventure—though sometimes he ends up covered in mud rather than glory! Whether it's lassoing raptors on the loose or helping a pterodactyl find her missing eggs, no job is too big—or too small—for Jon!

TANGO

Triceratops

Tango is the roughest and toughest triceratops around! She has a habit of acting without thinking things through, but together with her partner, Miguel, there is no problem that the two of them cannot solve. Just make sure you watch out when she is charging in to save the day!

CLOVER

Brontosaurus

Clover is a long-necked baby brontosaurus and Min's dino-partner. Although he can be clumsy, Clover has a big heart and loves to help Min take care of other dinosaurs on the ranch. Together they make an amazing dino-doctor team!

BLITZ

Velociraptor

The fastest dino in the herd, Blitz, a velociraptor, is a master of quick moves. As Jon's dino best friend, he's always there to back Jon up. But when he bolts, no other dinosaur can catch him. A terrific team, Jon and Blitz are "fast friends"!